Royal Rap

Written by Laurence Anholt

Illustrated by Alice Morentorn

Collins

It's time to stomp, it's time to clap.

Jump on the throne for the ROYAL RAP.

William the Conqueror, as everybody knows,

Won the **Battle of Hastings** with 10,000 bows.

William the Second (or Willy the Red)

Went out hunting, came home dead.

Henry the First was harsh but fair,

But he didn't have a son so he didn't have an **heir**.

Stephen danced in through the palace door

As the country exploded in **civil war**.

Empress Matilda was England's first queen.

She was cross and crabby and downright mean.

Henry the Second caused a holy **upheaval**

When he murdered a bishop in
Canterbury Cathedral.

Richard the First was the Lionheart Crusader,

Though his enemies called him
a ruthless invader.

John's **Magna Carta** was decent and good.

He was king at the time of Robin Hood.

Henry the Third served longest of them all.

He set up **parliament** in Westminster Hall.

Edward the First was brawny and brave,

Sent Robert the Bruce running – into a cave.

When his son Edward took his turn,

He was bashed by the Scots at **Bannockburn**.

Edward the Third then ruled the nation,

But the **Black Death** halved the population.

Richard the Second spent years in jail,

As Chaucer was writing a Canterbury Tale.

Henry the Fourth took the throne by force,

Caught a horrid disease and died, of course.

Henry the Fifth fought the Hundred Years War,

And defeated the French at **Agincourt**.

Henry the Sixth crowned at nine months old,

Was capable of miracles, so we are told.

Edward the Fourth was lofty and royal.

A man of peace and his people stayed loyal.

Edward the Fifth had eight weeks of power.

He was murdered with his brother in
London's Tower.

Richard the Third, with sword and shield,

Was the last king to die on the battlefield.

Henry the Seventh sure loved to spend,

As the **War of the Roses** came to an end.

No one liked food like Henry the Eighth.

He got through wives like he got through plates.

Edward the Sixth was next on the scene,

But he passed away aged just 15.

Mary the First was seriously scary.

She chopped off heads, did Bloody Mary.

Elizabeth the First was a royal success,

Known to her people as Good Queen Bess.

James the First, both English and a Scot,

Was the king who rumbled the **gunpowder plot**.

Charles the First wanted so much **tax**,

They cut off his reign with the swing of an axe.

Cromwell's Republic now appears,

And the royals take a rest for 11 years.

Charlie the Second liked to look pretty,

While the Plague and the Fire swept through the city.

James the Second was not liked much.

He ran for cover at the sight of the Dutch.

William and Mary shared the throne.

After Mary died, Willy ruled alone.

Poor Queen Anne was the saddest bride.

She had 17 children, all of them died.

George the First was a German duke.

His English sounded like gobbledegook.

George the Second was next in line,

German too, but his English was fine.

George the Third, he died insane.

15 children and a 60-year reign.

George the Fourth spent more than a million,

On fancy buildings like the Brighton Pavilion.

William the Fourth was ruler of the waves,

The Sailor King who freed the slaves.

Victoria's **empire** spanned the globe,

A sad-faced monarch in a **mourning** robe.

George the Fifth tried to help the poor,

Changed his name to Windsor in

the First World War.

Edward the Eighth was forced to flee.

They wouldn't let him marry a **divorcee**.

George the Sixth's stammer made him
difficult to hear.

In the Second World War he showed no fear.

Elizabeth the Second is the current queen.

What happens next remains to be seen.

These are the royals, both good and rotten.

Remember this rap and they won't
be forgotten.

Glossary

Agincourt: a village in France where Henry the Fifth famously defeated a large French army in 1415

Bannockburn: a town in Scotland where Robert the Bruce defeated the English in 1314

Battle of Hastings: the battle in which William the Conqueror defeated the Saxons in 1066

Black Death: a deadly illness that caused black spots on the skin

civil war: a war within a country between different groups or areas

Cromwell's Republic: when Oliver Cromwell became ruler of England as an elected head of state, instead of a monarch

divorcee: a person whose marriage has been legally ended

empire: a group of nations under one ruler

gunpowder plot: when some Catholics, including Guy Fawkes, plotted to blow up James the First in 1605

heir: the person who receives another person's property or title after that person has died

Magna Carta: the document signed by King John in 1215, giving English people freedom

mourning: sadness after someone has died

parliament: a group of people who decide the laws for the United Kingdom

tax: a sum of money paid to a government

upheaval: a sudden change

War of the Roses: the struggle for the English throne between the house of York and the house of Lancaster

Royal timeline

1066–1087:	King William the Conqueror
1087–1100:	King William II
1100–1135:	King Henry I
1135–1154:	King Stephen
1141:	Queen Matilda
1154–1189:	King Henry II
1189–1199:	King Richard I
1199–1216:	King John
1216–1272:	King Henry III
1272–1307:	King Edward I
1307–1327:	King Edward II
1327–1377:	King Edward III
1377–1399:	King Richard II
1399–1413:	King Henry IV
1413–1422:	King Henry V
1422–1461:	King Henry VI
1461–1483:	King Edward IV
1483:	King Edward V
1483–1485:	King Richard III
1485–1509:	King Henry VII

1509–1547:	King Henry VIII
1547–1553:	King Edward VI
1553–1558:	Queen Mary I
1558–1603:	Queen Elizabeth I
1603–1625:	King James I
1625–1649:	King Charles I
1649–1659:	Cromwell's Republic
1660–1685:	King Charles II
1685–1688:	King James II
1689–1694:	King William III and Queen Mary II
1694–1702:	King William III (ruled alone)
1702–1714:	Queen Anne
1714–1727:	King George I
1727–1760:	King George II
1760–1820:	King George III
1820–1830:	King George IV
1830–1837:	King William IV
1837–1901:	Queen Victoria
1901–1910:	King Edward VII
1910–1936:	King George V
1936:	King Edward VIII
1936–1952:	King George VI
1952–:	Queen Elizabeth II

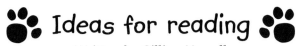

Ideas for reading

Written by Gillian Howell
Primary Literacy Consultant

Reading objectives:
- listen to, discuss and express views about a wide range of contemporary poetry
- discuss and clarify the meanings of words
- continue to build up a repertoire of poems learnt by heart
- explain and discuss their understanding of poems

Spoken language objectives:
- use relevant strategies to build their vocabulary

- give well-structured descriptions, explanations and narratives for different purposes
- participate in discussions and performances

Curriculum links: History

Interest words: conqueror, heir, upheaval, Canterbury, cathedral, Lionheart, crusader, parliament, brawny, halved, population, Chaucer, Agincourt, capable, gobbledegook, mourning, divorcee

Word count: 651

Build a context for reading

This book can be read over two or more reading sessions.

- Look together at the cover illustration and read the title. Ask the children to predict the content of the book. Ask them to explain what they know about rapping.

- Turn to the back cover and read the blurb to confi rm the children's predictions.

Understand and apply reading strategies

- Read pp2–3 to the children. Ask them to identify the rhyming words in each couplet.

- Discuss how the rhyming words do not always share the same spelling pattern, e.g. *red/dead, fair/heir, door/war*. Explain that the rhymes can help them pronounce new or unusual words.